GIANT JOURNEY

GIANT JOURNEY

by Steven Kroll
illustrated by Kay Chorao

Holiday House · New York

Library of Congress Cataloging in Publication Data

Kroll, Steven.
Giant journey.

SUMMARY: Magnolia decides to seek adventure in the
big city rather than marry Ignatius whom she considers
nice but ordinary.
[1. Giants—Fiction] I. Chorao, Kay. II. Title.
PZ7.K9225Gi   [E]   80-20512
ISBN 0-8234-0381-5

For my favorite giants: Margery, Jan, and John

Ignatius and Magnolia had been best friends and neighbors for five hundred years.

Every day they had lunch in Ignatius's garden, and went for a long walk in the village. Every night they sang to the music on Magnolia's record player. Then they went outside and looked at the stars.

One day at lunch, Ignatius looked up from his cheese sandwich and smiled. "Magnolia," he said, "why don't we get married?"

Magnolia was surprised. "What?" she said. "You mean after five hundred years you want to marry me? Well, let me think about it."

Magnolia went off to the woods to think. She sat down on a log and thought of how ordinary Ignatius was. He never made anything but cheese sandwiches for lunch. He never did anything exciting on their walks around the village. He never wanted to take her to a concert. And when they watched the stars, he never even held her hand.

"No, I will not marry Ignatius," Magnolia said to the trees. "I will go out into the world and find excitement!"

She went home and told Ignatius.

"I don't believe you," he said. "You must be joking."

"It's true," said Magnolia. "I'm going away."

Ignatius was so upset, he went straight to bed with a hot-water bottle.

Magnolia banged on his bedroom door. "You'll see!" she shouted. "You'll be happier without me!"

Ignatius hid under the covers.

Magnolia went back to her house and packed a suitcase. The next morning she left for the city.

The morning was sunny and warm. Magnolia walked and walked. She picked leaves off the tops of trees to fan herself. By the time she reached the city, she was very hot and tired.

"What I need is a good lunch," she said out loud to the crowded street.

And suddenly a gentleman giant was standing beside her.

He was wearing an elegant suit and polished shoes. He had a mustache and carried a cane. "Why don't you come with me?" he said. "I will take you to La Mélodie, the finest restaurant in our city."

"Oh," said Magnolia. "That would be lovely."

When they got to the restaurant, they were seated at a special table.

Magnolia ordered a hundred boiled trout, but when they came, she didn't know which fork to use.

"You're using the wrong fork," said the gentleman giant as she plopped the first fish into her mouth.

"Oh, I'm sorry," said Magnolia, seizing another fork, "I didn't realize."

"You're talking with your mouth full," said the gentleman giant, "and you don't have your napkin in your lap. I don't think I can stand this another minute."

And he left.

Everyone in the restaurant turned to stare. Magnolia was embarrassed. She wasn't hungry anymore, and she had to pay the whole check herself. Fumbling with her suitcase, she rushed out the door.

A few blocks away, she could see the park. A stroll among the trees would make her feel better. She hurried in that direction.

The trees were tall and shady. There were trim lawns and a large pond. Magnolia turned a corner and bumped into a skinny giant squinting through binoculars.

The giant looked up. He was wearing goggles. "What kind of bird are you?" he asked.

"Bird?" asked Magnolia.

"Yes, bird," said the giant. "Are you a penguin or a flamingo? Wait! You're an ostrich I once knew in Australia."

"An ostrich?" said Magnolia. "You must be thinking of someone else. I'm just a giant taking a walk."

"I'll walk with you," said the skinny giant. "But I hope you won't mind my bird-watching."

"I won't mind," said Magnolia.

They started down the path together. A moment later, the skinny giant crouched behind a bush and whispered, "Look, a scarlet tanager!" A moment after that, he threw himself on the ground and pulled out his binoculars. "Yippee!" he snorted. "A potbellied grackle!"

When this had happened several times, Magnolia stooped down and tapped her companion on the shoulder. "I'm not enjoying this walk," she said. "I don't want to walk with you anymore."

The skinny giant looked up. "Who wants to walk with an ostrich anyway?" he said.

Magnolia turned away, shaking her head. She hadn't gone more than a few steps when she heard the sound of a guitar.

A bearded giant was sitting on a bench playing the popular song, "Giant Rainbows."

Magnolia sat down beside him. "Do you mind if I join you?" she asked. "'Giant Rainbows' is one of my favorite tunes."

The bearded giant nodded, and Magnolia began to sing along. They sang one verse together and then another. It was nice singing with a real guitar, not just a record. Perhaps the bearded giant would invite her to a concert this evening.

All at once, the giant stopped playing. "You have a terrible voice!" he said.

Then he packed up his guitar and left.

Tears filled Magnolia's eyes. The sun was going down, and she had nowhere to go. She was alone and miserable.

But someone was prodding her. She looked down. A human was sitting a foot away.

"Hi," said the human. "My name's Calvin. Would you like to watch the stars with me? I love looking at the stars."

Through her tears, Magnolia said she would. Calvin was too short to take her hand, but together they walked into the middle of a field.

"I used to be with a circus," said Calvin. "I traveled all over the world. I rode horses and lived in a tent, and everyone bought tickets just to see me."

"How nice," said Magnolia. "But look at the *stars*, Calvin. Aren't they beautiful and romantic tonight?"

"I was a terrific clown too," said Calvin. "I wore all this funny makeup and ran around in floppy shoes and jumped out of tiny cars and had water squirting out of my head."

"Calvin," said Magnolia, "the stars—"

"I loved being a clown," said Calvin. "I loved making everyone laugh."

Magnolia slipped away. She ran across the field and out of the park and out of the city.

The world wasn't so exciting after all. Not when strange gentlemen couldn't stand your table manners and crazy bird watchers couldn't enjoy a walk. Not when guitar players were rude about your singing and humans could talk only about themselves. She missed Ignatius. She missed his cheese sandwiches and his quiet enjoyment of the things they did together. Most of all, she missed the way he loved her for herself.

She was still running when she reached his house. She threw open the front door and dashed up the stairs. The bedroom light was on. The bedroom door was open. Ignatius was still in bed.

Magnolia threw her arms around him. "I'm sorry, Ignatius," she said. "I love you, and I want to marry you."

The next day Ignatius and Magnolia were married.